I0571156

Puzzle
Pieces

Jasmine M. Powell

Copyright © 2018 Jasmine M Powell

All rights reserved.

ISBN-13: 978-0-692-10736-2

DEDICATION

I'd like to take this opportunity to thank all my loves who contributed in some way or another to the ideas for this book. I'd also like to thank my family for being so supportive and encouraging to me to finish this book.

CONTENTS

Introduction

Well, anyone who knows me knows this was a long time coming. I tried to find a way to have some of my poetry and some of my short stories in one book and this is what I've come up with. Each story is a companion to the poem immediately preceding it ...kind of...well, I just hope you all enjoy it. Probably won't be doing this again, HA HA.

Strange Path

Twisted walkways of my soul,

Here you meander.

Pacing the empty corridors of my mind.

Doubt and Need.

Obsession and Desire.

Inch by inch you insinuate yourself in my being.

Your essence woven into the fabric of my sanity.

With each step you take my mind breaks.

Fractures to re-purpose itself so I can see you

through a new lens.

Clarity and Hunger.

Focus and Thirst.

I can win this.

I can forget you.

The weight of it, my mind refuses to fathom.

I cannot fight my crazy without you.

Those hands on my skin pull me from the brink.

Teetering into mindlessness.

Almost lost to oblivion.

Two Sides

Her:

I can see him in my peripheral vision. He is sitting in the front row, behind my husband-to-be's head. His gaze is intense and I feel my abdomen clench. As the ceremony moves on, I shift slightly in my uncomfortable heels and fiddle with my bouquet. I wish it was over. Dear god, why did I want this type of display? And why the fuck would he sit in the front row? I realize I can look straight at him from the corner of my left eye while appearing to be looking at my fiancé. He's got on sunglasses. Dark ones. But I can still feel his eyes. There is a heat as they move up and down my body, lingering on my hips and cleavage.

Focus. I drag my eyes away from him and set them squarely on my almost husband, who is smiling and tearing up as the preacher drones on about some this, that or the other.

I smile back at him and let my eyes lose focus. Mr. Front Row is adjusting his pants leg. I sharpen my gaze to him as we move to the side for someone to read a piece of poetry. He lips his licks and smirks. My nipples harden and wetness seeps into my silk panties. My maid of honor reaches down to straighten my gown and a sharp tug on the back lets me know I'm being too obvious. I straighten up and turn to the poetess. When she finishes it is time for the vows.

I keep my gaze firmly on my fiancé, ignoring Mr. Front Row who is mouthing the vows in my peripheral vision. I slide the ring onto the thick finger and repeat after the preacher, the ache in my chest larger with each word. I'm sure people assume these are tears of joy and happiness. I close my eyes, kiss my husband and head off to take photos. The session helps me calm myself and serves as a reminder that I'm "doing the right thing."

Cheers greet us as we enter the reception hall and immediately work our way into our first dance. He whispers he loves me into my ear and I smile and hold him close. My heels have me slightly taller than him so it is a little awkward, but we manage. After the dance, we sit to eat, then move from table to table greeting our family and friends. People are starting to hit the dance floor by the time I reach my love. He asks me to dance and I agree.

A strong hand sits chastely on my upper back and his large hand encompasses mine as we swirl around the dance floor. We don't speak until he notices I am trembling.

"Relax…I won't fuck this up for you."

"I know…but…you know…"

"Yeah, I know."

He towers over me with my heels and the song is not long enough. I step back after a large inhalation of his cologne and he walks me back to my husband. I swallow back the tears and take a large gulp of rum to hide my face. I watch him walk back to his table and collect his coat before heading out the door.

Him:

I can't remember ever feeling this defeated. This angry. This lost. I stand stiffly, hiding my eyes behind shades as the woman I love marches down the aisle to marry someone else. I turn my head slightly to look at her future husband. At least he's good to her. It takes everything in me not to grab her hand and run when she reaches the front. But I behave and sit. I tune out the ceremony and focus on her. I can feel it the moment she sees me.

I can see her body react. The shortening of her breath and the parting of her lips. Why the fuck did I sit on the front row? Because I wanted her to see me. I wanted to make it hard for her to do this. Because it should've been me. How was I to know she wanted this? A regular life? Kids and work and bad sex. How could she want that when we make fire together? I curl my lip in disgust and shift my eyes down. Gotta control this. She doesn't deserve me to ruin her day.

When I look up again, I let my eyes roam over her body from head to toe. She can feel it. When I get to her hips, I stare hard at the cleft between her legs in the silken dress and she shifts her thighs apart slightly. I let my gaze continue upwards to her hardened nipples and frown. I can't have them anymore? Perfect sized chocolate drops. This is unbearable. I reach to adjust my pants leg as some fat bitch comes to read some stupid poem.

When I lift my eyes again the bride has her eyes on me. I lick my lips and smirk. She sways and the maid of honor moves to adjust her dress. That quick she snaps her eyes off me and it hurts.

I finish watching the ceremony wondering if the room can feel our tension. Our heat. I wonder if they think she's woozy for her husband. And not me. The wedding party recesses and I catch the maid of honor's eye as she leaves.

"Stop" she mouths and I nod in compliance.

I ignore the picture takers outside the church and head to the banquet hall. Music on the drive over helps me to calm down and my growling stomach gives me something else to focus on. I laugh when I see my table. To her right. Close enough for her to see me but far enough away that it seems respectable. I shake my head and sit down. Let the fucking festivities begin.

I ignore their first dance and get up to order a drink. How the fuck could she marry someone that small? It's like she purposely went and found my opposite. It's annoying. But not annoying enough to leave her alone. I couldn't anyway. She couldn't leave me alone either. Been there. Tried that.

I down a few drinks and sit to eat my food. I watch as they make their way to each table hugging family and friends and taking pictures. By the time they get to my table the dance floor is packed and a slow song is coming on. I ask her to dance and am surprised she says yes.

We move slowly around the floor. I keep my hands where they belong and inhale her perfume. It's a struggle not to crush her against my front. She's trembling.

"Relax...I won't fuck this up for you."

"I know...but...you know..."

"Yeah, I know."

The song is too short. I look down and see my emotion mirrored in her eyes. I sigh and walk her back to her husband, grab my jacket and leave. I text her from the car on my way home.

Twin Flames

Do you remember me?

I see you with my third eye.

I know your scent.

I know your hands.

I know your breath pushing into mine,

as you push into me.

I saw you and recognized you with my most secret

self.

The me that has traveled the universe lifetime after

lifetime.

Do you know me too? Have you forgotten this?

We were fire and ice.

We moved mountains.

We were magic.

I am drowning in you.

Broken glass strewn on hot coals… I will walk this

to make you smile.

Hungry. Feed me. All of you.

Let me devour your secrets, your wishes, your dreams.

Do you remember me?

We watched the rise and fall of nations.

Our bed cradled generations.

Why can't you see me?

My soul cries to your spirit. SEE ME!

Patience and obsession.

The inner me quivers when I hear your voice.

Tendrils reaching for the other piece.

Waiting, for you to remember me.

RECOGNITION

"Why am I here?"

I stir the small straw in my rum and coke and fan myself with a limp cocktail napkin. My friends are somewhere on the dance floor and I'm tired of trying to find them in the dark. The thin material of my purple dress is beginning to stain as I perspire more with each sip.

I order another and pretend to dig in my purse. Why the hell did I leave my phone in the car??? Sucking my teeth, I close my eyes as the music changes. The party beat replaced by something low and guttural.

When I open my eyes, there is a man standing to my left. Something about him places me immediately on edge. I sway on my stool and grab my fresh drink. As I lift the rum to my lips the man leans over the bar to place his order. I inhale and shift closer to him.

He smells like sex. There is something smoky and spicy in his cologne and before I realize it I'm touching his arm. He isn't startled.

"You wanna dance?" I ask.

Fuck these sweat stains. Before he can answer I walk towards the dance floor and turn to face him. He didn't follow.

Disappointed, I sigh and prepare to head back to the bar when I realize he didn't follow because he sat on my bar stool. To watch me. I lock eyes with him and the heat is so intense I almost look away. Instead I raise my hand to my thick curls and lift them seductively from my neck. As I begin to move my hips in a seductive wine, the guitar and the smoke voice on the track guide me.

I got caught out in the rain
If I die, I don't care I don't care
I'm in loooooove, I'm in loooooove

By the time the song ends I notice the people have moved around to give me space and watch. When I spy a few dollars on the floor I'm suddenly embarrassed. I want to go home. My friends appear and hustle me towards the bathroom asking how many drinks I've had. When I look in the mirror my spirits lift. My eyes are low and lusty and the red lipstick perfectly sets off the golden undertones in my chocolate skin.

Smiling, I adjust my dress and fluff my curly 'fro. As we exit the bathroom I sense him. A whiff of cologne…and I can feel those eyes.

"You wanna leave?"

I nod yes and ignoring my girls, I lean into him and we head to the door. He's tall and I fit snugly into the crook of his arm. The heat rises off his skin and I'm suddenly hungry for him. We don't speak in the car but his hand traces symbols of lust across my thighs as we head…wherever.

"You need a drink or something?" he asks.

"No, I'm fine, thank you."

When he parks I can't resist and get on all fours to lean over and kiss his neck gently. But he firmly pushes me back and turns to look at me. I understand. Not yet...but soon.

We enter a dark apartment and he directs me to the chaise. I lay back on it and he turns on some music. It's a continuation of the club. Low and sexy and dark. Tribal. My lips part and I dart my tongue out to wet them. Saliva gathers in my throat and I shift my thighs slightly, suddenly hoping my lack of panties won't leave a damp circle on the furniture.

He gets a chair and places it near the chaise. He leans back and stares over at me thoughtfully. I'm ravenous. I want him to hurry up. I want him inonpushingdeep. I shake my leg in irritation as he continues to stare. Finally, he reaches a hand over to quiet my leg. When he touches my skin, sparks fly from my knee to my thigh...then higher.

I part my legs slowly, searching his eyes. He tilts his head in acquiescence and leans back again. Frustrated I sit up and he motions me back.

"Lay back and entice me bitch."

Splash. I wriggle out of the dress and lay back on the chaise. I let my heels fall to the floor and stretch my purple polished toes. Slowwwwwwwwly I trail my hands up my thighs. Bypass where I want them most. Cover my stomach and bring them to my breasts. I rub them gently. Pinching and pulling my nipples to attention. They swell and plump with pleasure and I finally let a hand fall away to my pussy. I close my eyes and sigh softly as the hand traces the outer edges of that wet fold.

"Look at me."

I struggle to open my eyes. When they find his, I know they are screaming for him. He smiles. And does nothing. I'm annoyed now. I scoot to the edge of the chaise and spread my legs wide. Lift my feet to tiptoe and slide two fingers in my wet pussy. Before I can close my eyes again he is there, lapping my juice as it flows sticky and sweet. His hand lays flat on my stomach, pressing me down. I fall back and I'm already cumming. Thighs tremble as he does...something amazing to my clit. Some humming, wet, nibble tickly thing. I cry out and he moves fast. Shoving his tongue in my mouth for me to taste myself. His hands are everywhere. On my breasts, on my ass, slipping inside me.

I writhe beneath him. I am desperate for him. Something about his aroma...his presence... the music... his eyes... his touch on my skin... I need it. I beg for it. I reach for him.

He swivels out of reach and laughs in my ear. Speaking something foreign. French? Clarity begins to slide as I cum again, bucking hard against the palm of his hands.

I am tired of this now. I open my eyes to glare at him. He will recognize me now. He will give me this thing NOW.

"Ba'nmwen'l kounyea." I hiss.

His eyes widen. He sees me. He sneers and pushes my legs to my ears.

"Kounyea." He growls.

I let out an exhaustive groan as he enters me. There is no mercy. One hand grips my throat as the other spreads my ass apart. He mutters and bites. He stops to take my throat. I am insatiable. Thick saliva falls onto my breasts and I rub it into my nipples as he plunges viciously down my throat.

When he is hard as a diamond he flips me onto my stomach and falls atop me. His fingers gather a handful of my curls and yank my head back as he thrusts hard into me. I yelp and he laughs.

"Sa k'genyen? Kisa ki rive ou? I AM THE BARON! I AM KING HERE!"

He spreads my ass with both hands and moves slowly. Watching himself disappear into me over and over. I push back against him and wrap my feet around his knees which rest against the floor. He pulls. I push back. We fight this way for some time. When I can do no more, I fall limply to the chaise covered in sweat and my thighs sticky with my own cream. He comes for me again.

Kisses my thighs. My tender pussy. My stomach. My breasts. He bites my nipple hard and I cry out. He pulls my hair from my neck and bites hard there too. I pull his face to mine and kiss him as he opens my legs. I pull back. Tender now. We need to wait.

He smiles. Takes my wrists and kisses them before pushing them above my head.

"Slowly" I whisper.

His eyes find mine and he teases me there. Rubbing me with his dick until I am flowing again. And hungry. My hips stabbing into the air to catch him. He leans down and puts his lips to my ear. As he throughsts viciously he softly sings to me...

"Maman Brigite papa mouin té wè sa allan tou kaye la pa wè guin yin du feu map broté dlo pou mouin tuyé du feu map broté dlo pou' m tuyé du feu la pli pa tombé pa we terre a glissé.".

Savior

Murky waters.

My blood is cold sludge.

I shiver beneath the roots of my love tree.

Waiting.

Where is my sun? My sweet rain?

To ease upon my fetal-curved limbs may I rise like a

Golem from the mud.

I am lost.

Eternal REM.

Waiting.

But here… Here it now comes.

Warm rays caressing my soil and breathing life

upon me.

Soft rain soaking into my stiff limbs and

Tendrils sprout from my weary heart.

Grasping…Pushing…Clawing…Fighting my way

OUT

And here, on my knees, in the light of my sun…

I burn.

Molten lava.

My blood is hot fire.

I am feverish beneath the branches of my love tree.

Ready.

Where is my storm? My chaotic tornado?

Touches like glacier springs to quell this inferno.

Find me.

Eternal impatience.

Ready.

But here…Here it now comes.

Lightning strikes in the heart of my netherworld.

Torrential rain encasing my battered spirit.

Enchanting…Alluring…Disarming…

Winning my soul.

And here, in your arms, in the eye of my storm…

I breathe.

Love Song

I'm jarred awake by the acrid stench of cigarette smoke. My eyes water and burn as I gaze across the smoky room and smile. You sit hunched over the keyboard gazing absentmindedly out of the window. Ashes fall gently to the floor as you hum an unfinished melody.

"Good morning." I call.

You look over at me. Look through me, your mind a million notes away. I blow you a kiss and roll out of bed. As I get closer to you I see the dark circles under your eyes, notice the empty coffee mugs littered around your feet.

"You gotta sleep babe." I mutter, gathering the cups and heading into the kitchen.

You ignore me. It's going to be a long day. I'll need to leave so you can work. Or you'll be unbearable. Such is the plight of a musician's wife. I take my time washing the cups and pulling on jeans and a large sweater.

By the time I head out the door you have already forgotten I am alive. I twirl my wedding ring around my finger and try to figure out where to go. The library? The park? The mall?

I glance up at the sky. Cloudy. Might rain. I guess the library. As I head down the sidewalk, I think back to how we met. Years ago, I went out for karaoke with friends. We were munching on chips and salsa and knocking back shots of whiskey when the most beautiful voice floated into my ears. It wasn't just me. Every woman in that place turned to the small stage. And there you were. Hat pulled low over your eyes, mic resting easy in your left hand, crooning. I can't even remember what went through my mind but I remember walking away from the table and pushing my way past prettier women to get to the front. I placed myself right in front of you and gazed into your eyes as you sang.

Your voice reached into the bottom of my vagina and I was suddenly dripping down my leg. I imagined every position possible in that space of three minutes and it took my friends pulling me back to the table to snap me out of the trance you put me in. I wondered if you felt my heat. I tuned my table out as I watched you move through the crowd, accepting drinks and hugs. I wanted you. Bad.

It took me six months. Six months to learn your name and stalk you on social media and show up everywhere I might be able to hear your voice, and finally get an introduction through a mutual friend. I remember the first conversation was awkward and stupid. I couldn't stop staring at your lips and your voice made my mind foggy.

It wasn't until you tapped me on the shoulder a week later as I sat in the park at the water's edge, scribbling poems in my notebook that we actually hit it off. That first day we talked until dark. Didn't even get lunch or anything. Just sat in the park, on the grass, talking and laughing and falling into an easy infatuation.

I cross the street hurriedly, my mind still focused on us and our courtship. It was a whirlwind of bar dates and park outings. Wine tastings and karaoke nights. Singing gigs and poetry readings. And the first time we made love? Fire. We burned up the room with our passion and that never stopped. Even when you get in your moods. You still come to give me that feverish heat. That hungry, can't get enough, obsessive sex.

And we married. The same way we decided to vacation or quit a job or try something new… we woke up and ran to the courthouse and did that shit.

I've never been so happy. You complement and complete me in ways I still don't understand. And I love you for it.

I switch directions and head to the park instead, suddenly wanting to see where our journey really began. I seat myself on the grass and allow the memories to flow over me. Taking pictures in foreign countries. Getting in the car and driving until we get lost. Watching you create, your voice like silken honey in my ears.

I even revel in your frustration when you can't get the dreamt melodies out. My stomach growls and I glance at my watch in shock. It's late afternoon. I've lived a lifetime in one short day.

I enter the house and hum my way through the kitchen. The freshly washed mugs are now dry and I put them away slowly, listening for you in the bedroom. I hear nothing. I make my way to the doorway and peer in.

You are still hunched over the keyboard. Eyes closed. I steal over to you and lean down. You are cold. I close my eyes for the most painful memories.

I think of the first time I realized you weren't singing the love song to me but to someone behind me in the crowd. I could feel the energy between you two. I recognized it. It used to be mine.

I stopped attending your gigs. You were creating so much music. Endless love melodies seemed to circle through your dreams and pour into your keyboard. I cried silently in the kitchen while you whispered lyrics that weren't meant for me. So I crushed the pills. Night after night. Into your food, your coffee, your fucking cigarettes... until I could silence your voice.

Forbidden

Can caramel flavored kisses unlock the universe?

A galaxy contained in brown lips and firm hands.

Lips tugging mine and teeth nibbling me to ecstasy.

Quivering thighs and tingling toes.

Chocolate tongue and mocha lips.

No wonder Pandora opened her box to look at Eve's fruit.

Fingers clasp the tip of my soul and wiggle gently until release.

Cradled in your hands, sharing the same breath, archingpullingpushingaching.

Things to remember pushed into the darkest places as kisses soak into my interior.

Claimed kisses feeling inferior…to this.

Who knew caramel flavored kisses could unlock the universe?

Time

Youth

I close my eyes as his hands slide through my braids. Gently, he massages my scalp and I relax into him, my thigh across his legs and my head on his chest. Music plays softly in the background and we lay silently in the dark.

"What are you gonna do?" he asks

"I don't know... don't want to think about that right now."

He sighs and pushes my leg to the side. We shift in the bed until he's laying behind me with his hand cupping my hip. We've fallen asleep in this position for years, since high school. I close my eyes and snuggle backwards. But he is rigid. Stiff. Mad.

"What's wrong?" I whisper into the darkness.

"How long?"

"How long what?"

"How long do I have to wait for you?"

And there it is. The question he's asked me silently for seven years. Since I walked away the first time. And all the times since. I still have no answer. How can I explain this? That I only walk away because I know he's there for me to come home to? It sounds cruel. Selfish.

"I don't know" I finally respond.

I hold my breath as he processes my words. I can feel his body relax as he unwillingly accepts them. I breathe out and reach for his arm. He holds me. And I sleep.

The next morning I wake up to his face. His eyes are already open and he brushes my hair back as I blink the crust from my eyes. I smile and he pulls me over roughly. No good morning and he is sliding inside me. On my side, right leg slightly higher than the left, gripping my ass and pounding me. He smirks when I cry out and his hands slide up my body to trap my wrists. He leans into me and places his mouth next to my ear.

"I love you"

"I love you too"

He bites my ear and sits up. One hand curls around the top of the headboard and the other grips my ass again. No mercy from this angle. I cry and cum and plead and cum. When we finish I fall asleep, unable and unwilling to get dressed and leave.

"Get up… I gotta go to work"

I'm shaken awake a few hours later and stumble blurry-eyed to the bathroom to pee and wash my face. I make myself presentable and follow him to the car.

"You picking me up from work today?" he asks

"Yeah"

I turn on some love songs and lay back in the seat. When he puts his hand on my thigh, I reach a hand up to his hair and rub his scalp. His neck. His ears. Whatever I can reach. The drive is quick and I give him a deep kiss before watching him walk away. My phone rings as I pull off.

"Hey babe"

"Where you at?"

"Just dropped somebody to work…where you at?"

"Waiting for you to get here, I cooked."

"Oh ok… be there in a lil' bit."

A million thoughts run through my mind as I drive towards my boyfriend's house. Like they always do whenever I spend the night with my love. All the what ifs and should haves. All the I wills and I coulds. I push the litany of excuses away and hum along to the music. Soon I'm pulling up at my man's house and steeling myself for the barrage of affection he will give me when I ring the bell.

He greets me and I kiss him with my eyes closed, struggling to feel something…anything…but nothing. His hand on my back steers me into the living room where a glass of wine waits on the coffee table beside a plate of chicken and rice.

I eat silently as he chatters on. Finally, he pulls my foot into his lap and asks me about my day. I make up some fictitious work story as he rubs my feet and afterwards we watch a movie together as I sip my wine. My eyes keep jumping towards the clock as the time ticks by. Around midnight I stand up and fake a yawn.

"I gotta get home, work tomorrow and gotta make sure the kids get to school on time in the morning"

"Oh ok... you ok to drive?"

"Yeah, it was just one glass of wine."

"Ok babe, love you"

I smile in response and kiss him before rushing out of the house. I fly up the highway wiping away tears and wondering how I got myself into this mess. Bogged down with a man I don't love, sleeping with the one I do. I manage to get myself together before I pull up to Harris' job and slide over into the passenger seat. I must fall asleep because the next thing I know Harris is starting the car and placing his hand on my thigh. I smile lazily and curl my hand around his.

"You sleeping by me tonight or you going home?"

"Sleeping by you, my mama at home with the kids."

"Cool."

We stop for weed and beer and his disgusting cigarettes before pulling up to his house.

"Shit!" he curses.

"What?"

"My girl here"

"Oh…ok…I'll just go home then"

"Nah, hold on, just… go up the street right quick and let me get rid of her."

"Ok"

He heads into the house and I climb into the driver's seat. I pull up the road to the stop sign and wait. Five minutes. Ten minutes. Fifteen minutes. Twenty minutes. A text.

Meet me at the store in ten minutes.

I suck my teeth and head to the nearest corner store. While waiting, I run in and grab some candy, when I leave, he is leaning against my car. I smile and press up against him, relaxing as his arms pull me in close.

"She spending the night?"

"Yeah"

"So why you meet me at the store?"

"So I could say good-night"

"Mmmmmmm"

It's always like this. My man. His woman. Different names, same shit. Creeping around and being in love. I cling tighter to him for a few seconds before stepping back.

"You want a ride back to the crib?"

"Naw, I'll walk"

"You sure?"

"Yeah"

"Ok"

He puts a finger to my chin and lifts my lips to

his. It's a long kiss. A hungry kiss. When we break apart I get into the car and watch him walk across the street. He raises a hand as I pull off and I speed home jealous and angry. I wanted his hands on me tonight. I wanted to listen to him sleep. I wanted to wake up to him. I guess we don't always get what we want though.

Speed

I race across town in the middle of the night. The warm summer air whips my hair around and I mouth the lyrics to a slow jam. I'm almost on autopilot as I make my way towards Harris' crib, my eyes glazing over as I imagine his hands touching my skin. My phone rings.

"Hey babe." I feign interest in whatever my man is saying and lie about my whereabouts. As I've done an immeasurable amount of times this past two years. I hang up as I pull up to the curb beside Harris' house.

Before I can drop my purse he has me pinned to

the wall near the door. Kissing me. Soft lips gather my soul and prepare it for release. I moan as he bites my lip and kisses down to my breast.

A phone begins to ring. I focus enough to make sure it's not mine and wrap my arms around his neck. He lifts me towards the couch but we kind of stumble and fall to the floor close by. In seconds, he's lifted my dress and pulled my panties down.

I'm impatient tonight and only let him lick it up and down twice before I'm pulling him back up and into me. I whimper as he starts to long stroke my pussy into submission. I close my eyes and dig my nails into his back, shuddering as I cum. He flips me onto my side and bangs me into the floor until he explodes inside me.

After, we lay on the couch and I rub his back as I slip in and out of sleep.

"I'm getting married."

"What?!"

I sit up and look down at him. He looks back at

me gauging my reaction. The room dims a bit and I shiver. Panic seeps from my pores as I struggle to grasp how we got here.

"Um… congratulations?"

"You mad?"

"No…yes...I mean I don't know…I can't really be mad right?"

I'm rambling and I hate it. He reaches a hand to my lips and I flinch.

"This won't change anything really."

"Don't say that… it will… but that's ok"

I take a firm grip of my spiraling emotions and shove them down into my belly where they roil into nausea.

"You didn't tell… I mean… have you asked her yet?"

"Yes… last night… I wanted to see you before I posted the ring"

"Why? And why fuck me first?"

"Would you have still come to see me? Slept

with me?"

"Of course I would…"

"Don't lie."

"I would've come here and made you say it to my face."

My voice quavers slightly and I close my eyes against the tears. I'm going to lose him. I saw this coming. I saw how he looked at her when they met. I listened to his voice every time he said her name. I open my eyes.

"When?"

"She's setting the date and all that."

"Ok."

"Nothing's going to change!"

"Y'all gonna be living together how can it not change?"

"The fuck.. don't you live with your nigga? And manage to bring your fucking ass here when I ask you?!"

"Alright…"

I need to leave. I move to crawl over him and he blocks me.

"Please don't leave upset."

"I'm not upset."

"You are."

"I need to go."

He pulls me down and holds me. When the tears come he turns on some music and strokes my back until I wear myself out. This time he lets me dress and march to the car. I pull off without looking at him.

"You ok?"

"I'm fine"

I brush past my man and into the bathroom where I start the shower water. He comes up behind me and kisses my neck.

"I love you… you know that?"

"Yeah I know."

He kisses my neck again and lifts my head with his finger. My mind wanders as he gazes into my eyes. He tilts his head to one side and pulls me in for a hug.

"It'll be ok"

I push him away and step into the spray. I ignore his sigh and lather my body. Yeah. It'll be ok.

Distance

"Did you hear me?"

"I heard you."

I send a prayer of thanks up that my dark glasses cover my eyes and twist my ring around my finger. Marriage. What an in-the-way ass thing.

Harris lifts his glass of water to his lips and sips. Then he sifts through his fries and munches. I can't help the disgust brewing in my stomach. How can he eat? He's snatched my peace and left me teetering above chaos…. While he eats fries.

I sigh and gaze out of the window. The sun mocks my mood. A beautiful day gone to shit. Space my ass.

"So what kind of space and time do you mean?

Like… I can't see you every week so then what?
Once a month?"

He chokes and my heart stops. Nah. No. Not
this. I steel myself and don't look at him as he
speaks the words. He doesn't even have the decency
to stutter or stumble.

"I meant a real break babe… a couple months
maybe… shit is kinda sketchy at the crib and I need
to make her feel comfy."

I don't respond. He goes back to his fries. I feel
sick and bitterly wish I'd have kept the baby last
year. Disgusting. My ring twirls faster, flashing as it
catches the light.

Four years of marriage. Life comes at you fast.
My mind drifts back to the night Harris got
engaged. Then skips forward three months to my
own engagement. Ha! I purposely made my
wedding date the same day so I wouldn't think
about him as I said "I do." It didn't work.

"Ok… just hit me up when you… if you want to

see me… I've never wanted to ever disrupt any of your situations."

He leans forward and I shift my chair and look down at my hands.

"Babe…"

"Go settle your wife Harris."

I don't lift my head until his chair scrapes the floor. I can't look at him. Or I'll beg. I hate begging. He leaves. I raise my finger to order a drink.

Maturity

My foot hangs from the edge of the dock, my toes dipping down into the cold water. I shiver but make no move to head back to the house. My legs are bare in denim shorts but its early fall so they are safe from mosquitos. I roll onto my stomach and peer drowsily across the lake at the changing color of the leaves. I frame the shots in my mind but again make no move to grab my camera or phone from the house.

A slight shift in the atmosphere alerts me to his presence. I don't turn around as he drops down beside me and throws a sweater over my bare arms. We sit in silence, his fingers moving lazily through my braids, my foot making gentle circles in the water. We don't speak for a while and when we do talk it is about the beauty of the changing leaves, the quiet of the early morning, the desire to extend the peaceful vacation. I push away thoughts that extend beyond this day, this moment. The weekends here are always outside of time. Away from our real lives. Ignored phone calls in our hidden sanctuary for the past ten years or so. I know when we enter the house he'll make blueberry pancakes. I'll make bacon. I'll pretend I don't desire the hash browns that he hates. We will eat and then have hungry, passionate sex on the plush rug in front of the fireplace. As we have done every fall for years. But for now, we sit in silence, watching the sun climb higher in the sky, savoring each other's peace.

Us

Hidden words and patience.
Bitter words reside on love's tongue.

Play me a lullaby of submission.
Music stirs large appetites in the sea of my soul.

The walking dead are blind to passion's cry.
Sarcasm served with a glass of hot wine.

Restless inhibitions and dreams deferred.
Lost in Macadamia trees with white chocolate
blossoms.

Scarlett letters on chocolate skin.
Fire- red dragons with grey tongues roar whispers.
As they guard Rubik's cube hearts encased in a
Hadamard matrix.

Samson's strength launch Molotovs.
Shattered glass on bare feet.
Beneath it all ebony mermaids ride solid gold
waves.

Drown in oceans of forgotten words and cinematic
past time.
This is love.

FRIDAY: A PAYDAY SERENADE

I. The Addict

Have you ever been swimming and held your breath under water for as long as you could? Perhaps competing with someone? If you leave your eyes open, everything moves extra slow. But as you begin to run out of breath the pace quickens, almost in time with your lungs as they speedily begin to burn for lack of air. Finally, you burst to the surface and take that initial gulp of sweet air. You choke a little, maybe cough, but you feel that sense of relief sliding into your body as the goosebumps begin to appear on your arms. And then you do it again. My marriage is like that. I hold my breath as I rush to the finale, and then start the play again.

It's Friday. I drag my body out of bed and stumble into the bathroom. With a groan of sleepy annoyance, I struggle to unscrew the cap from the toothpaste and begin to brush my teeth.

As I scrape the disgusting plaque from all the crevices of my mouth, my eyes wander across my face. I linger on the areas of smooth skin and classic structure and skim the surfaces filled with disappearing scrapes and scars. After my makeup is done, I dress hurriedly and move into the kitchen. It is seven-thirty. Trey left for work hours ago. With a quick dip into the candy dish for a Lemonhead, I walk out to my car.

It's Payday. My heels click-clack through the halls of the school as I head to my office in the detention hall. At eight-fifteen a.m. Robbie Marshall is already waiting for me.

"Robbie, school hasn't even started yet!!"

"And?"

I grimace at his insolent tone and feel anger rippling low in my belly. Without a word, I pull his file and count his offenses. Three in the last two weeks.

"What did you do today?"

"Got in an all-tuh-ca-shun."

"With who?"

"Shenita."

"Your girlfriend?"

"Yeah."

"Did you hit her?"

"Naw. I pushed her into the lockers so she would shut up and Mr. Moody sent me over here."

The hair on the back of my neck lifts as I look at the fourteen-year-old in front of me. I recognize the threat of his cold eyes as he re-tells the story in more detail. The detachment in his voice and the stiffening of his body.

Suddenly afraid, I shout for him to stop and immediately send him off the main office. Attitude problems are one thing but fights are something else entirely. I glance at the clock. Time moves slowly.

It's Friday. I cram the last bit of salad into my mouth. The ranch dressing oozes down my throat and for a moment I struggle to breathe.

"You okay Marie?" Michelle asks. She teaches chemistry.

"Yeah, I'm fine, just got some lettuce caught in my throat."

"Oh…well anyway, thank God it's Friday, whatchu doin' this weekend?"

"You know Trey takes me shopping on Saturdays…and ain't nothin' good about Fridays."

"Girl you trippin'…getting away from these bad-asses for two days?!"

I just shake my head and don't answer. Instead my mind wanders to Trey. He could be finishing up his turkey and ham sandwich and heading back to work. As Michelle brings me back to my world with stories of her students I begin to clean up my trash. My hands shake slightly as I tip the bowl into the trashcan. I ignore it. Time always speeds up after lunch.

It's payday. I walk to my car after work. My feet are starting to swell inside my cheap pumps and I look forward to a long, hot bath. Loud laughter causes me to look towards the kids getting on the buses. I spot Robbie standing next to Shenita, his arm slung around her waist. Robbie catches my eye and smirks, his arm pointedly tightening around his girlfriend. I am embarrassed and quickly get into the car. I glance over one last time at the teens and Robbie gives me the finger. My cell phone rings on the way home and I answer.

"Hello?"

"Hey babe."

"Hey."

"I'ma be late tonight."

"You're late every Friday Trey" I respond impatiently.

I listen anxiously to silence before I realize he has hung up the phone. Biting my lip, I push the conversation from my mind and pull into the driveway. As my routine requires, I undress, run a hot bath and soak for fifteen minutes before standing up under the shower spray to scrub the residue of bath oils away. My eyes linger for a moment on a large purple bruise on my inner thigh and I caress it lovingly before turning the water off and getting out.

"It's Friday." I remind myself as I stir the rice and check on the chicken. His beer is waiting to be opened and poured, frosty and soothing, into a tall glass. My eyelid twitches when I glance at the clock. It's almost midnight. Moving into the bathroom, I take one last glance at my hair pinned into a bun and my flawless makeup. My robe hides a new pair of lace boy shorts with matching bra. I hear a car.

"One…two…three…" I start to count and run back to the kitchen. By the time I reach ten, the plate and glass of beer is on the table. I stand nervously over the sink of dishes.

It's Payday. Hot breath, reeking of tequila wafts over my neck. I cringe as his hand brushed my shoulder. My hands hang limp at my sides. My body is wound tight as a spring and I want to scream. I'm ready. The first blow knocks me into the fridge and I feel the tears behind my eyes. I begin to crawl towards the doorway. Instinct sends me to the left around him rather than through his legs.

Mistake. Now my head is ringing and blood flows freely from my nose. With strangled calls for mercy, I leap over the couch and throw myself towards the back of the house…he catches me.

"It's Friday." I whisper later as I slide into bed with him. I know he has already placed the money for tomorrow in my purse.

I wonder briefly how long our marriage will last and the answer frightens me. I wheel my mind away from that train of thought and snuggle my head into his arm. He does not apologize. I am not looking for his apology.

II. The Dealer

Remember the first time you swam to the deep end of the pool? You start out in shallow water and the anticipation leaves you feeling light-headed and nervous but you keep going. Half-way to the diving board you stop and look back. You realize you are in the middle of the pool. You've come too far to go back and have no choice but to keep swimming. Your arms are feeling a little heavy and your breath is kind of labored. A little snot is maybe running from your nose. But beneath this shaky, border-line exhausted exterior, you feel something rise unbidden and unexpected from your middle region. Pride, exhilaration, and fear all rolled into one.

Pushing thoughts of failure and drowning from your mind, you dive under and continue until you grip that hard, cool edge in your shaky hands. My marriage is like that. I swam out and now rest somewhere in the middle of the pool, waiting to grip that edge.

I love Fridays. I look over at the other guys getting out of their trucks. They hold coffee cups and bag lunches. I look over at my own bag lunch. Turkey and ham on wheat with a dab of mustard. Homemade coleslaw on the side with a slice of apple pie. On Mondays its tuna, on Tuesdays its roast beef. Wednesday is fried chicken and Thursday I eat out.

The same damn thing for five years. Many guys would kill for that type of stability, I just feel like I'm drowning in monotony. Shaking my head, I climb from the car and call hello to a few guys before whipping on my hard hat and getting down to business.

"I need a drink" I mutter as Bill calls me over. He's such an asshole. Sits on his fat ass in that air-conditioned trailer all day. Slaves us to death. Then has the nerve to do performance evaluations on Fridays. Like I'm some kind of weak ass office worker. I move away from the drywall work I'm doing and head over to him.

"How's it going Trey?"

"Alright."

"How's the drywall coming?"

"I only got two sections left to do."

"You know...on the last house you had the drywall done your first day out."

"The last house was about two thousand square feet smaller Bill."

"Of course, of course... just try to stay on task, there are plenty of Mexicans willing to do the job faster for much less money."

I grimace at his prejudice and look away. Bill chatters on for a few more minutes before latching on to another victim. I kick over a bucket of nails and get back to work.

Payday. I throw my sandwich in the trash and try to imagine what Marie would be doing now. Probably aping it up with some of her slut friends at work. I sigh and jog across the street to the deli. I feel adventurous and order a sloppy joe with chili-cheese fries. As the congealed mass slides down my throat I moan in culinary ecstasy. It gets no better than this.

"Hey T" Kevin sits down across from me.

"Wassup."

"What you doing tonight? Some of the guys are heading down to Rita's."

I smile at the mention of the club-slash-brothel and shake my head.

"Naw, I'ma grab a few drinks and then head on home...Marie and I have an...understanding about paydays."

Kevin laughs. "Yeah Shana and I do too... I bring home the check and she gives me some allowance...maybe."

I smile and pretend to enjoy his joke but I really wish he would leave me alone. He must have read my mind because soon he gets up to go, leaving me to my meal and a growing excitement.

"I need a drink." I say to Kevin as we are getting into our trucks.

"Yeah... you going to the bar?"

"Yeah, you?"

"Of course...meet you there"

Shortly, we are downing shots of tequila and guzzling Heinekens. My mind wanders as I consume alcohol. I feel the familiar anger grow. Who does she think she is? Why must she be so perfect with her lunches and her housekeeping?

What kind of woman works and manages to keep up with the house these days? Who does she think I am? Her and the smirk. I know what that look means. It means, "You're trash Trey." It means, "I wish I hadn't married you." It means, "What happened to all your dreams and goals?" It means, "What happened to the kids you promised me?" With a growl, I snatch another shot from the bar and gulp it down.

"Payday" I whisper, as I pull into the driveway. I know she is there, putting my plate on the table. Why isn't she in bed? Why must she make me feel so inadequate? I stumble into the house and ignore the carefully placed meal on the table. Marie is washing dishes and I take a moment to drink her in. She still has the same perfect figure I fell in love with. I know she is waiting for me. I move behind her and hover. I watch her hands tremble as she pretends to wash the dishes and feel my manhood stir.

Maybe we won't play the game tonight. I caress her shoulder and feel her tense up. She's afraid. Bitch. I smile and punch her into the refrigerator. As she scrambles across the floor I anticipate her moves. Suddenly she is sprinting towards the bedroom. I close my mind and catch her.

I love Fridays. I exit the bathroom. I listen for Marie. I don't hear her. I move over to her purse and slip in a few hundred bucks. This is why I stay. She knew how to play the game before I even knew what the game was…and I could never teach anyone else how to play. She makes me feel like a man. When she slips into the crook of my arm sometimes later I pull her close. I wonder if an apology is in order and then push the thought from my mind. She wouldn't like that anyway.

III. The Prey

Remember when you were younger and used to roughhouse in the pool?

You creep up behind someone and push them under for a few seconds and then swim away only to have someone push you under. It was all fun and games, but there was always the one kid who didn't know when to quit. Usually the biggest one of the group…a little bully of a shit. He would get ahold of your shoulders and plunge you under the water, maybe throwing his leg over you for good measure. As the seconds ticked by you would become more panicky.

You start to think of how to get this guy off of you. You begin to thrash, but that's what he's waiting for. So, the entire time you are under the water fighting for your life, throwing up promises to God, and trying to place a punch in this kid's nuts, he's up there laughing. Fucking laughing. He lets you go and you burst through the surface, gulping air. And then suddenly, you're his best friend and you're too scared to tell him to go to hell.

My marriage is like that. I was half-drowned into saying "I do" and now rest in a lifetime of fear.

I hate Fridays. I ease out of bed and tip-toe to the bathroom. My heart pounds when her arm moves. It eases when she does not wake. I pee. I wash up. I dress. I eat. Silently. I grab my briefcase and scurry to the car. My hand lightly brushes Marie's car in the shared driveway as I pass it by.

"I'm fine" I mutter when I trip on the curb. I enter my building and slide into my cubicle. I boot up my computer and fiddle with my stapler. I look at her picture and begin to sweat. My heart speeds up and I take my first glance of many at the clock.

"Good morning Andrew." I jump at Carol's words and give her a wave. She looks concerned. I immerse myself in paperwork.

"I hate Fridays." I exclaim and slide into the chair. It is our weekly productivity meeting. Someone will be let go. Someone will be promoted. I glance over at Carol.

She is filing her nails. I am filled with a sudden hatred for her and her perky morning chatter. I want her to be fired. Our boss enters and I regret my thoughts. Carol is fired anyway. I feel empowered.

"Sorry Carol, tough break."

"It's alright Andy, I got a better gig anyway."

"My name is Andrew."

She laughs and I want to push her down. Fear grips me and I hurry back to my cubicle and my computer.

"I hate Fridays." I type. I push send and the email goes to Henry. Henry is our top earner. He also hates Fridays. My eyes drift again to the clock. Again to the picture. I stare at her brown eyes under perfect eyebrows. I grimace at her sharp, white teeth. I imagine puppet strings on my arms. I hate her.

"Me too." I read. I glance over at Henry. He is taking a call. I too must appear productive and pick up the phone. As if on cue, calls trickle in and I am flooded in customer care.

"I'm fine." I whisper into the bathroom mirror. My eyes are read and my skin ashen. My cracked lips beg for chapstick. I wet my face and head to lunch. I sit down and order a tuna sandwich.

"You order the same thing every Friday."

"I know Henry."

"Goddamn…you don't get bored with that shit?"

"No"

"How's Kels?"

"Fine"

"She still up at the firm?"

"Yeah"

"Hmmm…so no kids for you guys hunh?"

"Not likely."

'Well…Barb just found out she's preggers again."

"What's that? Five now?"

"Damn right! I need all the bonuses I can get!"

"Umhm"

I bite my sandwich and the tuna slides down my throat easily. I chomp and swallow. Henry talks and talks. I don't interrupt. I never do. Henry finally heads back to work. I close my eyes and prepare my mind for her.

"I hate Fridays." I murmur as I pull into the driveway. Two cars. I park and enter the house. She is waiting on the couch.

"How was your day?" she asks.

"Fine." I reply.

She is wearing the black negligee. I imagine trailing her stockings across her throat and pulling...hard. She smiles. She motions for me to sit with her. I ignore her and go into the kitchen. There is no meal. I always cook. I sigh and begin to prepare dinner. Why can't she cook just one night? Why can't I pick out my own clothes?

Why must she decide who our friends are and what parties to attend? Why can't I visit my mother in the home? Why can't she choke on this chicken and die?

"I'm fine" I reply as I slide between the sheets. She rolls over to me and begins to kiss. I can't breathe. Her tongue winds into my mouth and steals my air. I push her and toll over. She grunts and lies still. I hear the car pull in. I hear Trey enter the house upstairs. I begin to sweat. I can feel her body humming with passion. I am disgusted. As the screams begin, she flips me over. Our sex is violent. With each plea from upstairs I thrust

"Take me" she screams.

I do not reply. I give it to her. Tears fall for Marie. Tears fall for me. Why won't she leave him? Why won't I leave her? Marie whimpers. I sob. Trey laughs. Kelly moans. I push her off, run to the bathroom and vomit into the toilet.

"I hate Fridays" I whisper. I sit in my armchair. I listen at upstairs. All is quiet. I listen for her. She sleeps. I imagine my life without her. Ambling. Shiftless. Worthless. Free. I tip-toe to the bedroom. I look at her. I pick up the pillow. I hover. I sigh and get in the bed. I cannot win without her. She conquered me.

IV. The Predator.

Do you remember strutting your stuff at the pool? Or was it the beach? You purchased the perfect bathing suit to out-do your peers and friends. You only went to the pool with your uglier friends. Or the less well-to-do ones with the shabbier suits from last year. You arrived and looked around for your target. Ahhh...there...the loser. Standing pathetically on te outskirts, waiting for you to draw them in. You would be their sun. They would orbit you. You smiled. You enticed. You insinuated friendship.

They didn't know you were a spider preparing for a meal. After a few comforting words and jokes you pounced. They didn't even register the change. You ordered. You dismissed. You beckoned. You hated them for their lack of self-esteem. You loved them for their adoration of you. This is what my marriage is like. I found my slave and reside in a temple of never-ending worship.

"I love Fridays" I chirp. I rise and dress. Andrew left for work ages ago and I'm glad. He's an annoyance. I sip my coffee and watch the news. My heels tap the floor. I am anxious for my day to begin. I rinse my cup quickly and head out to the car. Marie is leaving for work. I ignore her. She reminds me of Andrew. I cringe at the thought of his weakness and drive off.

"Come." I wave my secretary into my office and close the door. I toss a stack of unfiled reports onto her lap. She glances around nervously. I look out the window, hands clasped behind my back. I wait.

"I was going to get to them today" she begins.

"These reports are two weeks old Julie."

"I know Mrs. Steele, I'm just having so much trouble at home— "

"Julie?" I cut her off.

"Yes Mrs. Steele?"

"What are the duties of your job?"

"Ummm…answer the phones, handle the mail, greet clients, file reports…"

"I see…so…if you were me…and your secretary was never at her desk to greet clients, mis-delivered mail, missed calls and forgot to file reports…what would you do?"

"Ummm…I'm not sure."

I sigh and turn around to face the pitiful specimen Julie has become. I raise an eyebrow. I wait. She fidgets. I wait. She coughs. I wait. Motionless.

"I guess I would fire her."

"Good I expect your resignation letter on my desk within the hour, have a good life Julie."

I disregard her cries of protest and motion her out of the door.

"I love Fridays" I whisper to myself. I glance quickly over our weekly scores. I am impressed with my own numbers. My gaze wanders around my office. There are no family photos. No smiling children and no supportive husband. I like it that way. Show no weakness to the other losers at my job...and children smell bad anyway. I look at the clock and a tingle begins in my mid-section. It is almost time.

I cross over to the small sofa in my office and sit. My mind wanders to Andrew. My mother told me to find a weaker man. My mother said he will make your dreams come true. My mother was wrong. She forgot to teach me to mold him. To force him to fulfill those dreams. Weak men can't compete at work. They can't compete at home.

They can't handle social situations alone. I frown and imagine life with Trey. Marie is all wrong for him. Weak. Ineffectual. Submissive. He needed a tiger. He got a mouse.

"Come" I motion to Helen, my temp. She walks in, dropping her completed tasks on my desk. I pause to admire her shoes before firing off more tasks for her to complete. I realize she has no pad and pen and ask if she needs one.

"No ma'am."

"You remember all that?"

"Yes ma'am."

"Write it down anyway."

"No thanks and if you excuse me, I have to continue with your work."

My mouth drops open as she breezes from the room. What gall. She better have it all complete or I'll give her the worst recommendation of her life. But if she does… she's hired.

I need everything associated with me in this place to ooze confidence and competency.

"I love Fridays" I toast, downing my glass of wine in one gulp. Kenny is chattering on with the client. I ignore them both. Client-Kiss-Assing is not one of my job descriptions. Once the contract is signed I can give a damn about client happiness. Our contracts are carefully worded to make it much more touch to break than to sign your name.

"So Kelly, how is the project coming?" Kenny asks.

"And what project would that be Kenny?"

"Ha ha ha, Kelly you're such a jokester why… Mr. Lattimore's project of course."

I sigh, smile my most cruel smile and reply "I wouldn't know, you forget, I just find the clients, I don't tend to the menial task of completing their projects."

Before they can respond, I stand and walk out of the restaurant. I wonder what Andrew is doing. Probably eating his little tuna sandwich in a quiet corner of his cubicle. I shake my head. I wonder if my marriage is worth it and head back to work.

"Come" I beckon to the child across the parking lot. She skips over and I pass her the melted candy bar from my glove compartment, grimacing as her fingers touch mine. I head into the house, skirting around Marie's sad excuse for a vehicle. I enter the house and drop my purse to the floor. I begin my Friday routine of self-indulgency. I soak in the tub. I polish my nails. I put on my black negligee. When finished, I put on some jazz music and pour a glass of wine.

"I love Fridays" I whisper as Andrew gets into bed. I reach for him and he stiffens. I ignore his reluctance and kiss his body awake. Above our heads Trey has begun to beat her.

I tingle as her pleas for mercy become louder and louder. I moan as the thumps and grunts from above bring the animal out of Andrew. He dominates me. I scratch him. He holds me down. Trey punches. Marie screams. I come. Andrew vomits.

"Come" I mumble. Andrew does not hear. He hovers with the pillow. I know he will not strike. I wait for him to climb into bed. He cries. I wait. He mutters. I wait. He sleeps. I sigh and imagine life without him. I wish he wasn't so easy. I wish we had love.

ABOUT THE AUTHOR

Yesterday I walked in the sun.

Golden rays warmed chocolate skin.

But my spirit was still cold,

Shielded in icy layers of despair.

Hope came in the form of caged bird song.

It echoed from the hilltop.

It pierced my heart.

Beautiful notes from imperfect tongue, moved me to no

end.

Tears fell as ice melted.

Arms raised to rejoice.

The song cried "Live,"

And my soul wept.

---Jasmine Powell, *Caged Bird Song*.

I'm just a woman that loves to write. I have an unhealthy obsession with zombies and I love to eat. I love my kids and my family and I wish you all peace and prosperity. Thank you so much for taking time to read something so special to me.

www.ingramcontent.com/pod-product-compliance
Lightning Source LLC
Chambersburg PA
CBHW020550130626
46552CB00007B/2840